Illustrated by
Mira Ko

THE GLOOMY LIGHT
Sal & Ernie's Adventure

By JOSHUA ALEXANDER, ZA'METRIA FRONEBERGER,
DANA JONES, and KYARE TURNER

Reach Education, Inc. | Washington, DC

Reach: Books by Teens
Published by
Reach Education, Inc.
www.reachincorporated.org

ISBN: 0615884652
ISBN-13: 978-0615884653

DEDICATION

We would like to dedicate this book
to true friends.

In beautiful Rio, there were two loving friends named Ernie the Llama and Sal the Frog.

Ernie and Sal had been friends since birth. Every day when they were young, they would take a walk together to the park.

Sal would swing on the monkey bars and Ernie would catch him.

When they grew older, they went to school together.

Ernie was good at reading and languages (he could talk to BOTH humans and animals) and Sal was good at climbing and math class.

Every time a big final came, they helped each other study with their weaknesses and strengths.

When Ernie and Sal got older, they stayed good friends. Ernie had a wife named Shay, and Sal had a girlfriend named Lisa.

Nevertheless, they still spent time together. They took a relaxing walk to their favorite pond every night.

Ernie had a child on the way, and Sal could not be happier for him.

Because they were so close, Sal was going to be like an uncle to Ernie's child.

One misty Friday night, Sal and Ernie took a walk to the pond. They were lying on the grass relaxing, discussing how excited Ernie was to be a dad soon.

All of a sudden, they saw a great green gloomy light in the sky. They did not know what was going on. An image of Ernie appeared inside the gloomy light.

Slowly the picture drifted into letters and then into words.

It read: "We want you."

Ernie asked aloud, "You want me for what?!"

The light flashed off, and the sky went black. Within seconds, the light reappeared.

"Sorry about that," it now read. "We want you to teach us how to speak."

As the light came down, they tried to run away fast, but it quickly absorbed Ernie.

As Ernie was disintegrating into the sky, he yelled out, "My baby!"

Sal was so surprised he put his hands on his head and opened his eyes wide.

As he was raising his hands, he realized that he had turned green! (Whenever Sal gets nervous, he changes colors, and he was very nervous.)

When he uncovered his eyes, he saw a huge spaceship with a sign on it that said, "TO OUTER SPACE," like a sign on the front of a bus.

The baby was due in three days. What would Ernie's family do if Ernie were stuck in outer space? It broke Sal's heart to think of Ernie's new baby without a father. Sal really needed to find him.

For the next three days, Sal asked for help from random animals.

First he went to the beach, and he found a black and pink anaconda that was 30 feet long. His name was the Slithery Anaconda.

As Sal approached the snake, he turned neon blue. He was very nervous.

"Do you know how to get to outer space?" he asked.

"Sssssssorry," the Slithery Anaconda replied. "I'm not sssure how to get to outer sssspacccccce. But I can take you to the sssssscary jungle."

So Sal went to the jungle. He looked up and down, left and right to find someone to help him. Finally, in the highest tree of the forest, Sal spotted a toucan, whose name was the Screaming Toucan. He hopped from branch to branch to get to him, but the Screaming Toucan flew to the next tree.

Sal yelled after him, "Wait, wait! I need your help!"

The Screaming Toucan flew by him, and Sal yelled as he went by, "Do you know how to get to outer space?"

"I DO NOT KNOW HOW TO GET TO OUTER SPACE! BUT I HAVE BEEN TO THE TALLEST TREE IN RIO!" the Screaming Toucan squawked.

"GET ON MY BACK, I WILL TAKE YOU TO THE WISE MAN OF THE JUNGLE WHO MIGHT BE ABLE TO HELP."

Sal hopped on the
Screaming Toucan's back.
Together they flew up
to the tallest tree in Rio.
The sun was setting.
It looked as though it would
disappear forever, and the
trees were lit up from behind
as if they had a magical glow.

When they reached the top of the tallest tree, Sal was surprised to find a house that was made of wood. The house was very small and had one window, and a lamp was hanging just outside the front door.

When Sal hopped up to the front door, the door slowly creaked open. Sal walked in and saw a very old monkey with a cane.

"This is about your friend Ernie the Llama, isn't it?" the Old Wise Monkey said.

"Yes," Sal said. "Do you know how to get to outer space?"

"The button lies within the statue that flies," the Old Wise Monkey replied. He chuckled and laughed.

Sal did not know what to do, so he turned gray. "Thank you," Sal said to the Old Wise Monkey. "I have heard of a big statue on top of a mountain in Rio. Is that where I should go?"

"Maybe it is, maybe it's not. The only way to find out is to get to the top!" the Old Wise Monkey replied.

Sal hopped across random cars and then up a steep narrow road until he found his way to the massive statue that rose above the city.

The statue was of a man about hundred feet tall with his arms spread wide.

He knew he had arrived at the right spot as he turned back to his original color, muddy brown.

He hopped around the base of the statue and found a door on the left leg. He opened the door and hopped in.

When he got inside the statue, he found a sign that said, "TO OUTER SPACE." He also saw a big red button that was bigger than him.

"The button lies within the statue that flies," repeated Sal.

He continued to jump on the button until it pressed, and as soon as it pressed, he heard a rumbling voice yell, "TEN SECONDS TO TAKE OFF!"

A helmet appeared in front of Sal, right next to a sign that said, "Have a safe journey." He put the helmet on his head and it shrunk to his size.

Sal changed green as he quickly took a seat and closed his eyes.

10-9-8-7-6-5-4-3-2-1

BLAST OFF!!!

Sal's body fell back and his face fell forward. Before he knew it, when he opened his eyes, he was in outer space. He felt lighter than he had ever felt on earth. It was an awkward feeling.

Inside the statue was a window that looked out into space. When he looked out, he saw a spaceship flying next to him and as soon as he saw it, he knew it was the one that Ernie was in because it had that same sign that said "TO OUTER SPACE."

He found the door that would let him outside the statue and floated towards the spaceship. He felt so light he could fly. He was so relieved that he turned back to his original color.

When Sal got close to the spaceship, he heard the sound of an engine starting. Because he was a frog, he could use his sticky feet to attach to the slick metal sides, and he held on until the spaceship reached its next stop, Planet Slimeball.

Slowly the door to the spaceship opened, and the aliens appeared. They had four legs and were bald, short, green, and oozing goo.

It looked like they were having a conversation, but they were silent as church mice and it was obvious that they couldn't talk. Sal watched them ooze by and then he hopped into the spaceship.

Sal quickly looked around for any sign of Ernie, but he had no luck.

He looked high and saw a ceiling dotted with bright lights. He looked low and saw his own tiny little feet. He looked left and saw open doors to rooms that he searched.

When he finally looked right, just when he was about to give up, he saw furry ears that reminded him of Ernie. It was him!

Sal was so happy, he turned rainbow!

"Ernie!" Sal said.

"Sal!" Ernie said. He was strapped down to a table so it was hard for him to turn to see his friend.

"What are they doing to you?" Sal asked.

"No time for that," Ernie said. "We have to act fast. There is a teleporter hidden deep inside the ship that can take us home. We have to get the keys from the aliens!"

Just then they heard the aliens oozing past in the hallway. They also heard the distant jiggle of keys.

Sal had an idea. Finally his changing colors could be useful!

"Wait, where are you going?" Ernie asked as Sal hopped to the door.

"Don't worry," Sal said.

He changed to the color of the alien's slimy goo and oozed his way towards them. Cautiously, he grabbed the keys and oozed his way back to Ernie, without the aliens ever knowing a thing.

Now all they had to do was get to the teleporter.

"Hurry up, Ernie!" Sal said as he unstrapped Ernie. "Your baby could be born any minute!"

With that being said, Ernie took off!

They turned into narrow hallway after narrow hallway, until they finally found the teleporter at the very end of the last hallway they took.

Sal inserted the key, and immediately the spaceship said something in a language Sal could not understand. But Ernie could!

He mumbled something back to it, and the doors opened wide for them to enter.

Just then, the aliens arrived. They reached their slimy legs through the door to the room. They tried to shout angrily, but they could make no sound. Ernie finally realized why he had been taken: the aliens couldn't operate the whole spaceship without being able to speak.

If they had only asked me, I would have been happy to teach them, he thought to himself.

Suddenly, there was a giant rumbling inside the teleporter.

Ernie held on tight, but Sal accidentally flew against the wall.

"Why does this always happen to me?" he said.

About four minutes later, they finally arrived on Earth. Ernie thanked Sal for risking his life to save him.

"You're welcome," Sal said. "What do you think true friends are for? Now hurry home and go meet your new baby!"

They hugged goodbye and went their separate ways.

That night,
Shay had her baby.

And Sal and his girlfriend came to Ernie and Shay's barn to celebrate.

They spent the whole night talking about their adventures.

When Sal and Ernie went back to their favorite pond, they did the things they did when they were younger. They felt relieved to have a normal day.

The End

Acknowledgments

In July 2013, fifteen students embarked on an exciting journey. Tasked with creating original children's books, these young people brainstormed ideas, generated potential plots, wrote, revised, and provided critiques. In the end, four amazing books were created, showing again what teenagers can do when their potential is unleashed with purpose. Our fifteen authors have our immense gratitude and respect: Joshua, Jordan, Rashaan, Za'Metria, Marc, Sasha, Dana, Rico, Sejal, Angelo, Sean, Brandon, DaQuan, Kyare, and Zorita.

We also appreciate the leadership provided by our instructional leaders: Kaitlyn Denzler, Andrea Mirviss, and Brian Ovalles. Jusna Perrin, in addition to leading a team of teen writers, steered our summer program ship, seemingly with ease.

We also owe great thanks to our talented illustrators, Lucia Liu and Mira Ko, whose beautiful drawings brought these stories to life. And, most of all, we thank our dedicated and inspiring writing coach, Kathy Crutcher, who led our teens from the excitement of brainstorming through the hard work of revision to make these stories the best they can be.

Once the books were finished, publication costs could have made it difficult to share these stories with the world, so we appreciate the financial support provided by the New York Avenue Presbyterian Church, the Carr Family, the Denzler Family, Helen Runnells DuBois, the Hollowell Family, the Mirviss Family, and Cheryl Zabinski.

Most of all, we thank those of you who have purchased the books. We hope the smiles created as you read match those expressed as we wrote.

About the Authors

Joshua Alexander is 16 years old and is from Washington, DC. He likes to draw, sleep, watch TV, and go outside. He might want to be an artist. He goes to Perry Street Prep.

Za'Metria Froneberger is 15 years old. She goes to Perry Street Prep and wants to be a pediatrician. She likes to cook, run track, and make people laugh. SWAGG.

About the Authors

Dana Jones is 17 years old and goes to Perry Streep Prep High School in Washington, DC. She likes to do hair and hang out. She also likes to play and work with little kids. When she grows up, she wants to be a hairstylist.

Kyare Turner lives in Washington, DC and goes to Eastern Senior High School. He is 16 years old. He has a great imagination and loves baseball and track. He wants to own his own mechanic business because he loves cars.

About the Illustrator

Mira Ko is a student at VCUarts. Someday she would love to work behind the scenes at an animation company or as a children's book illustrator. She loves to shoot photos, go on adventures, skate, and spend time with loved ones. More of her work can be found at mirako.carbonmade.com.

About the Story Coach

Kathy Crutcher has mentored young writers since 2003 and is passionate about empowering others to tell their stories. After coaching the teen tutors of Reach Incorporated to write their first four books in 2013, she was inspired to found Shout Mouse Press, a writing program and publishing house for unheard voices. To learn more, visit www.shoutmousepress.org.

About Reach Incorporated

Reach Incorporated develops confident grade-level readers and capable leaders by training teens to teach, creating academic benefit for all involved.

Founded in 2009, Reach recruits entering 9th grade students to be elementary school tutors. Elementary school students average 1.5 grade levels of reading growth per year of participation. This growth — equal to that created by highly effective teachers — is created by high school students who average more than two grade levels of growth per year of program participation.

Reach creates readers. Reach creates leaders. And, by lifting two populations through a uniquely structured relationship, Reach is effectively attacking Washington DC's literacy crisis.

During the summer of 2013, Reach launched a new program to build on school year gains made by program tutors. As part of this program, teens partnered with professional writers and illustrators to create original children's stories. These stories, written entirely by our teens, provide our young people with the opportunity to share their talents and creativity with a wider audience.

By purchasing our books, you support student-led, community-driven efforts to improve educational outcomes in the District of Columbia.

Learn more at www.reachincorporated.org.

CPSIA information can be obtained at www.ICGtesting.com
Printed in the USA
BVOW07s0812260116

434212BV00002B/13/P